ROSS MacDONALD

HENRY'S HAND

GLUF

ABRAMS BOOKS for YOUNG READERS
—NEW YORK—

For Lucy, Jamie, Daisy, and for spare-parts people everywhere.
And for Chris Mulligan, a special soul, 1994–2012.

—R. M.

The illustrations in this book were made with watercolor and pencil crayon.

MacDonald, Ross, 1957–
Henry's hand / by Ross MacDonald.
p. cm.
[1. Hands—Fiction. 2. Monsters—Fiction. 3.
Friendship—Fiction.] I. Title. PZ7.M1513Hen 2013
[E]—dc23
2012039257

ISBN: 978-1-4197-0527-4

Text and illustrations copyright © 2013 Ross MacDonald
Book design by Ross MacDonald and Chad W. Beckerman

Printed and bound in China
10 9 8 7 6 5 4 3 2 1

Abrams Books for Young Readers are available at special discounts when purchased in quantity for premiums and promotions as well as fundraising or educational use. Special editions can also be created to specification. For details, contact specialsales@abramsbooks.com or the address below.

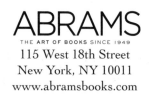

ABRAMS
THE ART OF BOOKS SINCE 1949
115 West 18th Street
New York, NY 10011
www.abramsbooks.com

Some of us start out whole and stay that way.
Some need a spare part or two.

Henry—he was a bits-and-pieces kind of guy.

Every once in a while, one of his bits would go astray.
One morning he left one of his pieces in the bed,
which made for a very *awkward* day.

And once, one of his eyes rolled under the couch and wouldn't come out until bedtime.

So Henry made up a little rhyme,
to help him take inventory every morning.

Of all his parts, Henry's right hand
was his favorite.

Henry and Hand did
everything together.

And went everywhere
together.

They especially loved the springtime, when it started to warm up, leaves began to bloom, and the birds got busy.

But sometimes, when Henry was feeling lazy, he would get Hand to do things he really should have been doing himself.

It's not that easy for a little hand to scrabble all the way down the driveway to fetch the newspaper every morning.

Or start the car when it's cold outside.

Henry was doing less and less, and Hand more and more.
And before long, Hand started to get more and more annoyed.

So one night at bedtime, when Henry sent Hand
to fetch his toothbrush,

Hand just . . . took off.

Henry didn't notice until early the next morning.

When Hand didn't come back with the newspaper, Henry knew right away that something was up.

Henry looked everywhere for Hand. At first he needed him. Then he started to miss his friend. Perhaps he was lost, Henry wondered. Or maybe even hurt.

After a while Henry realized that Hand wasn't coming back.

And it was all his fault.

Meanwhile, Hand headed off for the city—
leaving Henry to take care of himself.

Hand hitched a ride on the back of a turnip truck . . .

And by noon he was right in the heart of downtown.
The lights! The noise! The bustle and hubbub!
It was all so new and exciting to Hand.

He'd never felt more alive!

But by dinnertime he was cold, tired, hungry, lonely, dirty, scared, and ready to go home.

And that's when it happened . . .

Hand later said it was one of those
right place, right time kind of things.

Anyone would have done what he did.

But the papers didn't see it that way.

It didn't take long before Hand landed in the lap of luxury.

No more dirty country shack — Hand now lived in a big house in the best part of town!

He no longer had to wait on Henry hand and foot. In fact, the house was chock-a-block with butlers and cooks and maids who all waited on *him*!

He even had a room full of assistants to answer all the fan mail he had started getting. Hand didn't have to lift a finger!

But Hand soon found himself with nothing to do—every last thing was already being done by someone else.

Oh, sure—they'd give him little chores to "help," but he could tell that they didn't really need a hand with anything.

So, in a busy house filled with busy people in the middle of a busy city, Hand felt all alone.

One day, Hand spotted a bedraggled
little tree on the corner, with new buds
turning green on the ends of its branches.
It must be spring! he realized.

A small blue bird was trying to build a nest. But every time a big truck drove by, the wind would blow the nest apart.

The poor bird kept trying over and over, but she was getting nowhere. Hand wanted to help, but he just didn't feel like himself somehow.

His secretary was talking to him, but he hardly heard her.

Meanwhile . . .

Henry had his good days and his bad days, and he did his best to keep himself busy. It wasn't easy.

Spring was coming, and there was a lot of work to do.

He had to tend his garden.

The roof needed patching.

It was time to shake out the rugs and clean the house.

And there was always so much paperwork to do!

One day Henry was making breakfast when he heard a knock at the door. At first he didn't know what that noise was, since he never got any visitors.

But he soon figured it out.

And that . . . was that!

That's just how it is with old friends. You pick up where you left off. And don't need to say much.

A word here and there speaks volumes.

Spring arrived. It started to warm up. Leaves began to bloom, and the birds got busy.

So Henry and Hand took a walk to their favorite tree.